·TITCHYWITCH·

To Jenny

A Beaver Book
Published by Arrow Books Limited
62-5 Chandos Place, London WC2N 4NW
An imprint of Century Hutchinson Ltd

London Melbourne Sydney Auckland
Johannesburg and agencies throughout the world

First published by Hutchinson Children's Books 1987

Beaver edition 1988

Set in Century Schoolbook by
Rowland Phototypesetting (London) Ltd

Printed and bound in Singapore
by Tien Wah Press Pte Ltd

ISBN 0 09 957210 9

·TITCHYWITCH·

Jean Baylis

BEAVER BOOKS

One afternoon at tea time Sally Smith looked out of the window and saw the most extraordinary sight. Through the sky flew three witches on broomsticks. And on the middle one sat a tiny little witch holding on to her hat in the wind.

'Mum!' screamed Sally Smith. 'Come and look. There are witches flying through the sky and they're coming this way!'

'Don't be silly,' called Mrs Smith from the kitchen. 'You really must learn to stop making up stories.'

But Sally Smith knew what she had seen with her own eyes and if you read this story you will find that every word she said was true.

‘Here we are,’ said Warlock, getting off his broomstick. ‘Number 22. Not bad, is it?’

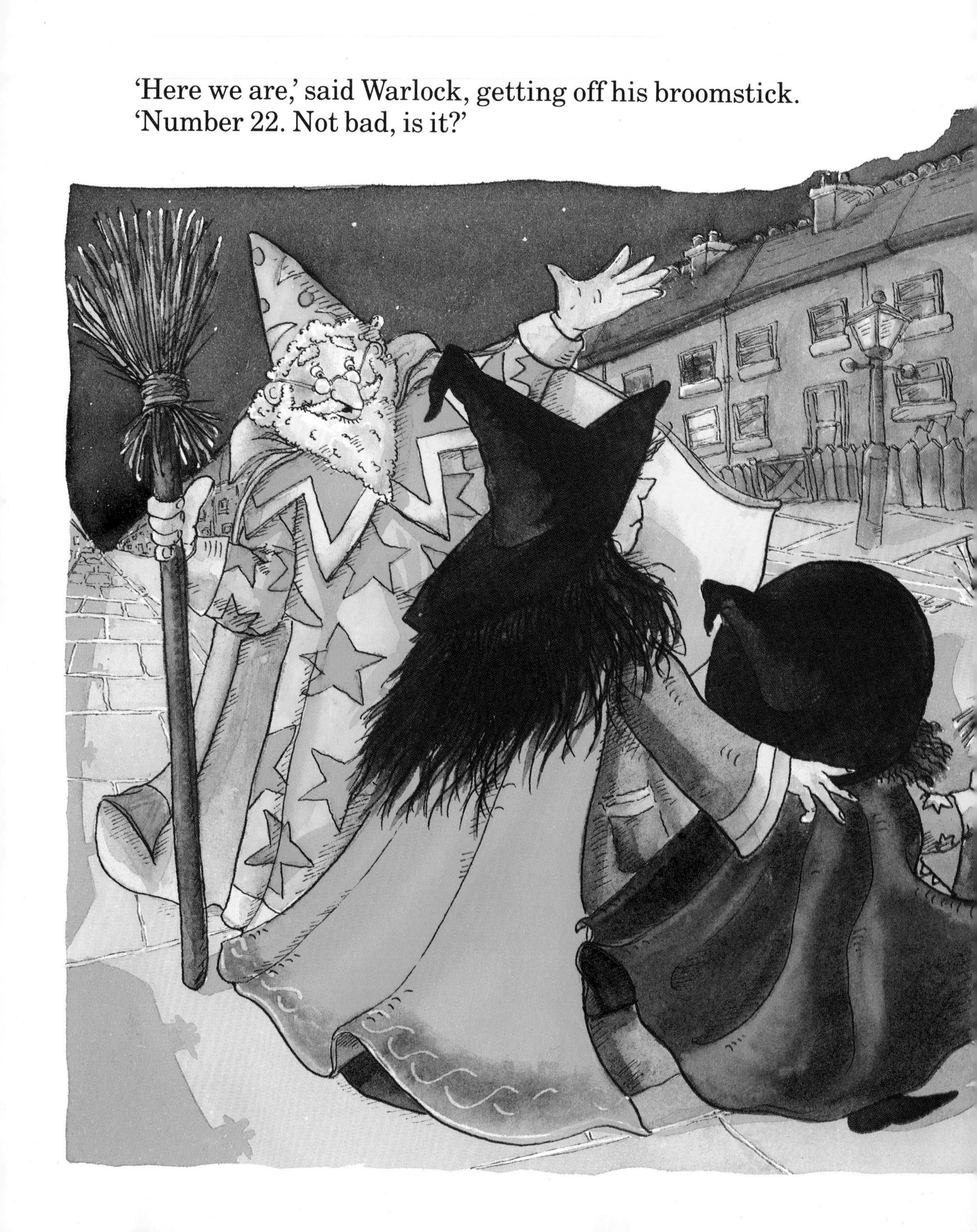

Titchywitch pulled a face. ‘Well, I suppose it’s all right for a *house*,’ she said. ‘But it’s not half as nice as our cave.’

‘No,’ said Big Witch with a sigh. ‘But now they’ve cut down our forest and built a road over our home, we’ll just have to try to live like humans. And that’s that.’

The family walked into the kitchen. Titchywitch gasped with disappointment. 'But it's horrible! There're no spiders or bats, or anything.'

'Never mind, never mind,' said Warlock, who seemed to be rather more pleased with the house than anyone else. 'We'll have it looking like home in no time.'

Usually witches sleep in the daytime and go out on their broomsticks at night. But that evening Warlock announced that they would all go to bed at night, just like humans. Titchywitch sulked all the way through supper and refused to eat her snail shell and nettle soup. She was absolutely certain she would never, ever, like living in a house, even if she lived to be 932 years old.

Lying in her hammock, Titchywitch found it impossible to sleep. Mum and Dad could pretend to be humans if they liked. But she was going out on her broomstick, and that was that.

Sally Smith was lying in bed when she heard a voice coming from the next door garden.

'Double bubbles, boils and troubles,' it said. She put her slippers on and crept downstairs and into the garden.

Standing on her toes, she looked over the top of the hedge. There was a tiny little witch standing in the garden. 'I knew it!' she said to herself.

Sally crawled through the gap in the hedge. ‘Are you a real witch?’ she asked.

‘Of course,’ replied Titchywitch crossly. ‘And I suppose you’re a real human.’ She poked Sally with her finger. ‘You’re all warm,’ she said.

Titchywitch explained about the house and how she hated it. And how everything was the wrong way round and back to front.

‘I’ve got hundreds of troubles,’ she said. ‘I was just doing a spell to turn them into toads, when you interrupted me.’ She held up her arms.

‘Double bubbles, troubles be toads.
Double bubbles, toads be troubles.’

All of a sudden the garden was full of slippery, slimy toads, croaking at the tops of their voices.

'Now I can fly off on my broomstick,' she said. 'If you promise not to tell, I'll show you how.'

Titchywitch took Sally into the garage. There were two big broomsticks side by side. 'These are Mum's and Dad's,' she said. 'Mine's only a baby one, but it can go quite fast. Do you want to go for a ride?'

'What, now! In my nightie, at *night*?' asked Sally Smith.

'Of course,' said Titchywitch. 'But as there are two of us we'd better go on Mum's. I know how to ride it.' And before she knew what she was doing, Sally was sitting behind Titchywitch on the big broomstick.

'Stars and moon and night-time sky,
Make my broomstick fly, fly, fly!'

And Big Witch's broomstick rumbled and shook and zoomed off into the sky at astonishing speed.

Up and up they flew. 'Oh dear,' said Titchywitch. 'It's going too fast.'

'Make it go slower!' said Sally.

'I'll just twiddle this thing,' said Titchywitch, turning a knob on the front. But the broomstick seemed to go even faster and soon they were so high above the clouds that they couldn't even see the earth.

'You don't know how to work it, do you?' screamed Sally, almost in tears.

'No, not really,' admitted Titchywitch. 'We're in trouble now!'

Round and round they whooshed like a rocket on fireworks night. Sally had a sick feeling in her tummy like the time she went on the big dipper at the fair.

Then, all of a sudden, Titchywitch called out,
'I've remembered!'

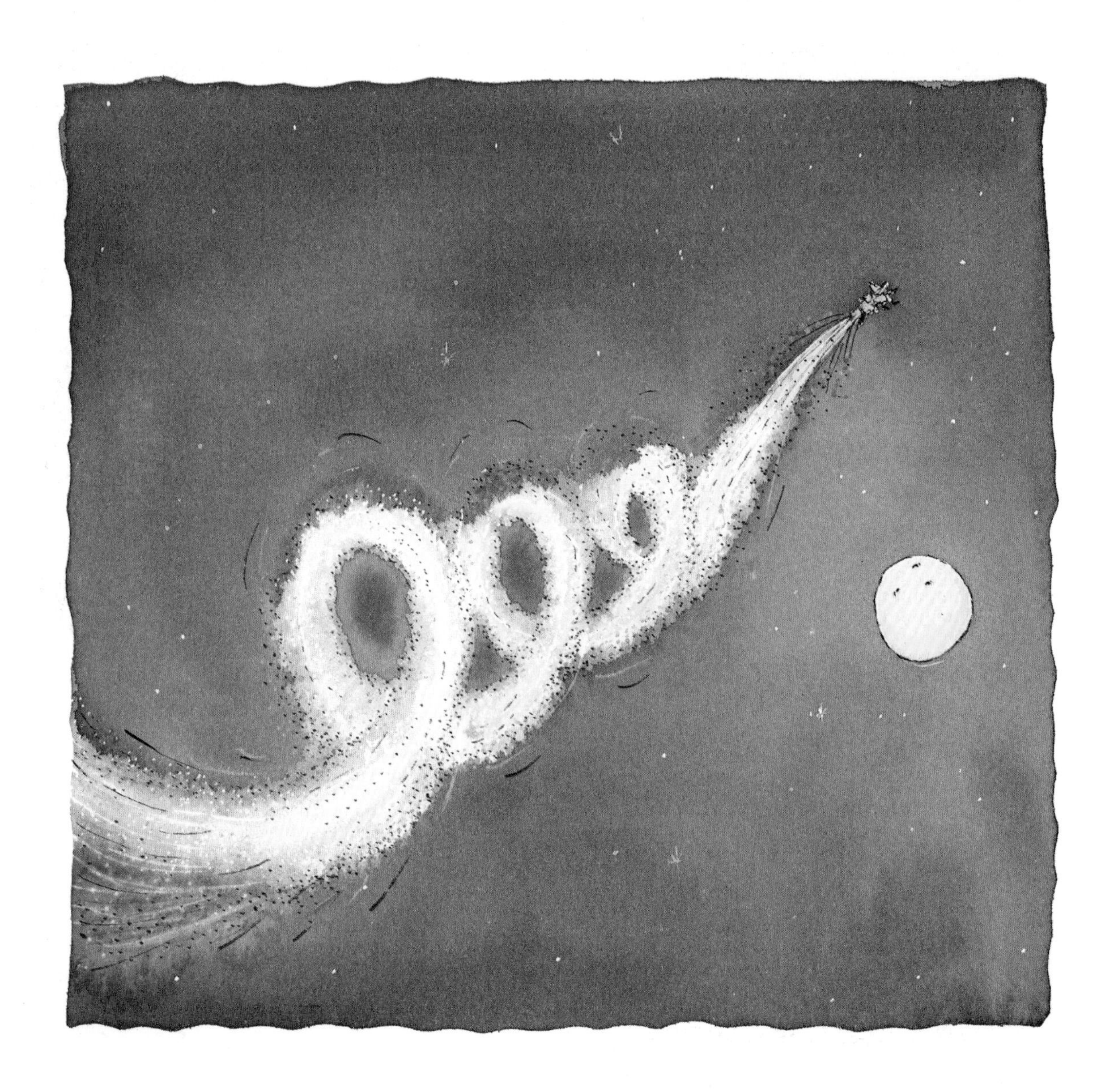

She pulled the brake. The broomstick rattled and shook, slowed down and steadied itself. The girls had a chance to look around.

'Ooh,' gasped Titchywitch. 'I've never been up this high before.'

They were so close to the stars they could almost touch them. Down below they could see the lights of the town twinkling. It was lovely.

Once Titchywitch had mastered the broomstick it was great fun. They went backwards and forwards, forwards and backwards. Then they tried flying upside down.

‘Can we fly to my house?’ asked Sally. ‘So I can wave to Mum.’

Back on earth, Mrs Smith was putting away the dinner things when she happened to look out of the window. She blinked once and she blinked twice. Had she really seen Sally flying past the window? ON A BROOMSTICK!

'Oh, dearie me!' cried Mrs Smith, rushing out of the door in her slippers. Outside the most astonishing sight met her eyes. On the pavement stood a witch, and by her side a big warlock.

'Come down at once,' he shouted, waving his cloak about furiously.

'That's my Sally up there,' screamed Mrs Smith. '*Do* something!'

But the broomstick kept on going. Up and up and then down and down and round and backwards and sideways and forwards.

'There's nothing for it,' said Big Witch quietly. 'You'll have to use the spell.'

'Moondust, stardust above the town,
Catch these girls and bring them down.'

He threw up his arms and a great whoosh of pink stardust shot up into the sky, enveloped the broomstick and gently carried the two naughty girls down to earth.

They landed with a bump in Mrs Smith's front garden. Sally looked up at Mum. 'I told you there were witches living next door,' she said.

Then everyone started to speak at once. No one noticed Titchywitch and Sally creep off by themselves to the back garden. There wasn't a toad to be seen.

‘Looks like all my troubles have gone’, said Titchywitch, ‘now that you’re my friend.’

And suddenly she thought it wasn’t going to be so bad living in a house after all.